GRRRRRRRRRrRGRrrrrGRr

This book is dedicated to our moms.
Thank you for all your help and support.
We love you.
—Daniel and David

www.randomhouse.com/kids/

Library of Congress Cataloging-in-Publication Data
Kamish, Daniel. The night the scary beasties popped out of my head / Daniel and David Kamish.
p. cm. — Summary: When nightmare creatures come to life and start to eat his toys,
Dan the Man battles the Beasties with his Mighty Pencil and wins.
ISBN 0-679-89039-4 (trade) — ISBN 0-679-99039-9 (lib. bdg.)
[1. Nightmares—Fiction. 2. Dreams—Fiction. 3. Monsters—Fiction. 4. Drawing—Fiction.]
I. Kamish, David, ill. II. Title. PZ7.K12685Ni 1998 [E]—dc21 97-31367

Printed in Singapore

10 9 8 7 6 5 4 3 2 1

Dan's peaceful sleep was jostled by a growling in his melon.

The growling
grew to RUMBLING,
and the RUMBLING
grew to SNARLING,
and the SNARLING

grew to
ROARING!

Dan grabbed his Mighty Pencil, and he drew the nightmare Beastie.

It POPPED right from his melon
onto the pad of paper.

If Dan erased the Beastie drawing, all the GROWLING, all the RUMBLING, all the SNARLING, all the ROARING would come SCREECHING to a stop and he could sleep.

But before he could erase it, strange moonbeams lit
the page and sparked life into the scary nightmare Beastie.

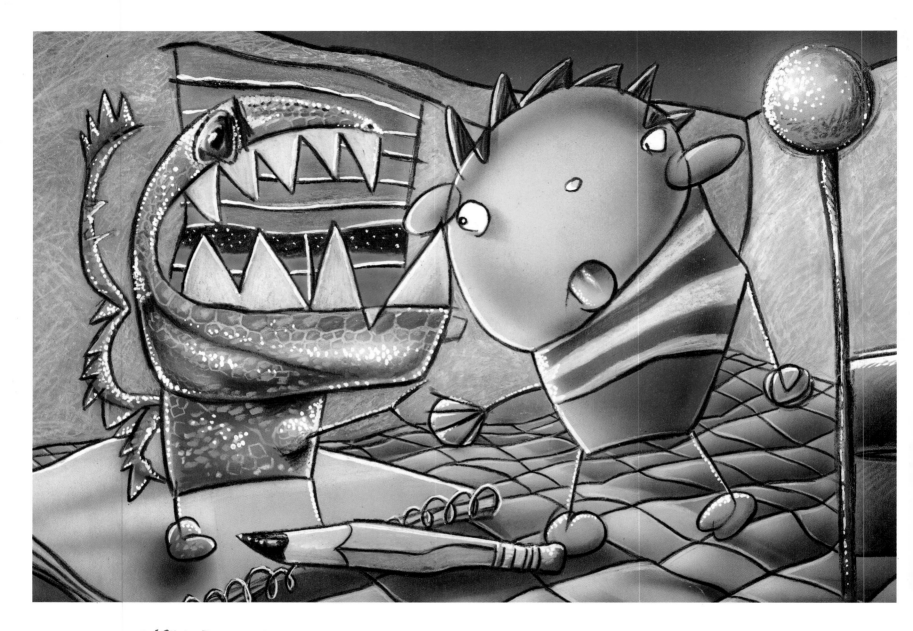

YOW! It POPPED right off the page and flashed its real Beastie teeth. Then the Beastie started GRUNTING and A-COUGHING and A-WHEEZING, and he SNEEEEEEEZED a Boogieman right out of his nose.

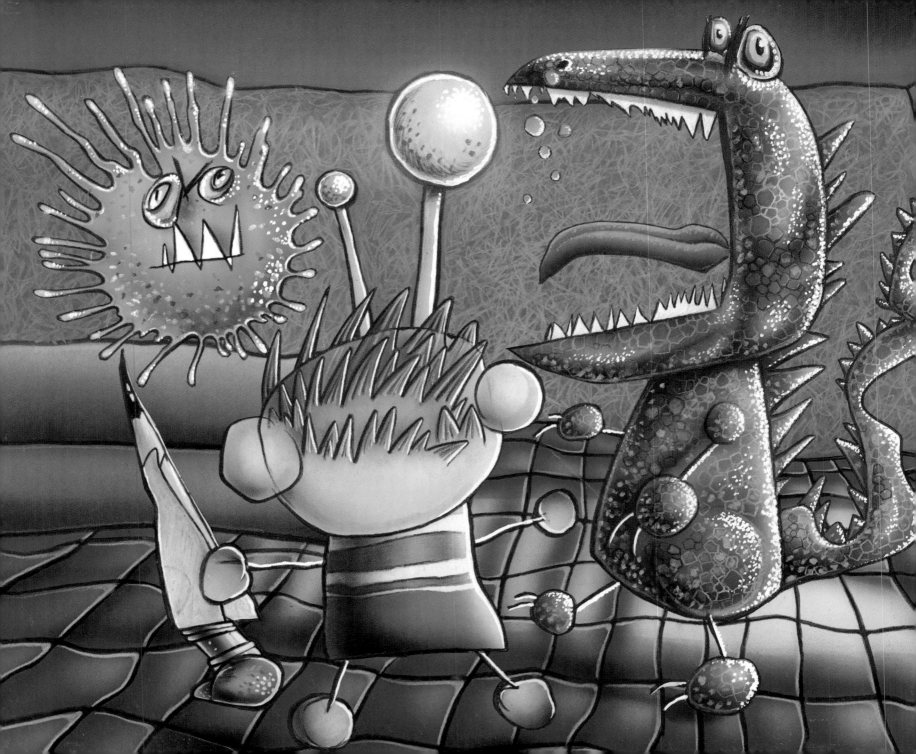

Dan now stood face to face with the Boogie and the Beast!
He politely said, "We could be friends and play with toys—
or watch the late, late show."

But nightmares aren't friendly. The Beastie ate the television ...
and gulped Dan's new Red Racer down his Beastie throat.

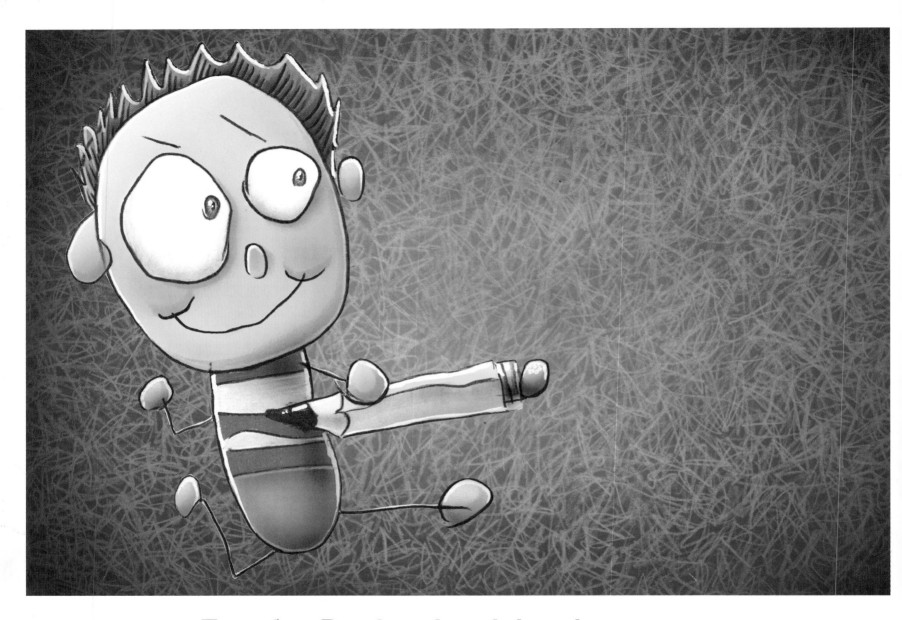

Eraser-first, Dan charged to rub the nightmares out.
But they grabbed his Mighty Pencil, drew a pencil
of their own, and escaped into the starry, starry night.

Dan needed help… and fast. So he drew a six-legged dog—
two extra legs for speed—to chase the nightmares down.

But the nightmares still were faster on the motorcycle they had drawn.
Dan felt like screaming! But instead of getting mad, he designed a clever plan.

The dog gave six thumbs up
as Dan drew a fire engine—
and off they raced to wash
away the nightmares.

The Beastie drew a fortress and a moat with toothy creatures.

HA! That didn't scare Dan—he knew he had them now!
It was time to send his nightmares to the showers.

As Dan soaked the nightmares down, the Beasties ROARED one final Beastie ROAR. But the ROAR shrank to a SNARL, and the SNARL shrank to a RUMBLE, and the RUMBLE shrank to a GROWL. The nightmares fizzled out…

...and puddled at Dan's feet.

As Dan erased the night away, the soft hues of morning warmed the sky.

With a calm head and a plan,
Dan had battled nightmares…and won.
He will no longer be afraid of
Beasties GROWLING in his melon.

But he keeps his Mighty Pencil close, just in case.

SWeet
dreams